Rumer Godden

Candy Floss

RUMER GODDEN
CANDY FLOSS

ILLUSTRATED BY NONNY HOGROGIAN

PHILOMEL BOOKS • NEW YORK

Text reprinted from *Four Dolls* by Rumer Godden.
The collection copyright © 1983 by Rumer Godden.
Candy Floss copyright © 1959, 1960 by Rumer Godden.
Copyright renewed 1987, 1988 by Rumer Godden.
Reprinted by arrangement with Greenwillow Books,
a division of William Morrow & Company, Inc.
First published in 1960 by The Viking Press.
Portions of this book were originally published in
1959 in *The Ladies Home Journal*.
Illustrations copyright © 1991 by Nonny Hogrogian.
Published in 1991 by Philomel Books,
a division of The Putnam & Grosset Book Group
200 Madison Avenue, New York, NY 10016. All rights reserved.
Printed in Hong Kong by South China Printing Co. (1988) Ltd.
Book design by Nonny Hogrogian
Lettering by Dave Gatti
The text is set in Bembo

Library of Congress Cataloging-in-Publication Data
Godden, Rumer, 1970–   Candy Floss / by Rumer Godden;
illustrated by Nonny Hogrogian.   p.   cm.
Summary: A doll named Candy Floss is very happy serving
as Jack's lucky charm at his stall at the fair,
until a spoiled rich girl steals her.
ISBN 0-399-21807-6:
[1. Dolls—Fiction.   2. Fairs—Fiction.   3. Behavior—Fiction.]
I. Hogrogian, Nonny, ill.   II. Title.
PZ7.G54Can   1991   [E]—dc20   90-19469   CIP   AC
First Impression

For Jane, who thought of it. — R.G.

This is the tune Jack's music box played

Once upon a time there was a doll who lived in a cocoanut shy.

You and I can say we live in London, or Chichester, or in Connecticut, France, Japan, Honolulu, or the country or town where we do live. She lived in a cocoanut shy.

A cocoanut shy is part of a fair. People come to it and pay their money to throw wooden balls at cocoanuts set up on posts. If anyone hits a cocoanut off the post he can keep it. It is quite difficult, but lots of nuts are won, and it is great fun.

9

This particular shy was kept by a young man called Jack.

There are many cocoanut shies in a fair, but Jack's was different. It had the same three-sided tent, the same red and white posts for the nuts, the same scarlet box stands for the balls; it had the same flags and notices and Jack called out the same call: "Three balls f'r threepence! Seven f'r a tanner!" (A tanner is what Jack called a sixpence.) All these were the same, but still this shy was different, for beside it, on a stool, Jack's dog sat up and begged by a little mechanical organ that Jack had found and mended till it played (he called it his music box). On top of the box was a little wooden horse, and as the music played—though it could play only one tune— the horse turned round and round and frisked up and down. On the horse's back sat a beautiful little doll.

The dog's name was Cocoa, the horse's name was Nuts, and the doll was Candy Floss.

A fair is noisy with music and shouting, with whistles and bangs and laughing and squeals as people go on the big wheel, the merry-go-rounds, or on the bumper cars. Jack's music box had to play very loudly to be heard at all, but Cocoa, Nuts, and Candy Floss did not mind its noise; indeed, they liked it; no other shy had a music box, let alone a dog that begged, a horse that frisked, or a doll that turned round and round. A great many people came to Jack's shy to look at them—and stayed to buy balls and shy them at the nuts.

"We help Jack," said Candy Floss, Cocoa, and Nuts.

Jack was thin and dark and young. He wore jeans, an old coat full of holes, and an old felt hat; in his ears were golden rings.

Cocoa was brown and tufty like a poodle; he wore a collar for every day and a red, blue, and white bow for work. Cocoa's work was to guard the music box, Nuts, Candy Floss, and the old drawer where Jack kept the lolly (which was what he called money). Cocoa had also to sit on a stool and beg, but he could get down when he liked, and under the stool was a bowl marked "Dog" and filled with clean water, so that he was quite comfortable.

Nuts was painted white with black spots; his neck was arched and he held his forelegs up. He had a black-painted mane and wore a red harness hung with bells.

Cocoa and Nuts were pretty, but prettiest of all was Candy Floss; she was made of china, with china cheeks and ears and nose, and she had a little china smile. Her eyes were glass, blue as bluebells; her hair was fine and gold, like spun toffee. She was dressed in a pink gauze skirt with a strip of gauze for a bodice. When she needed a new dress Jack would soak the old one off with hot water, fluff up a new one and stick it on with glue. On her feet were painted dancing shoes as red as bright red cherries.

The music box played:

Cocoa begged, Nuts frisked, Candy Floss turned round and round. All the children made their fathers and mothers stop to look. When they stopped, the fathers would buy balls and if anybody made a nut fall down Jack handed out a beautiful new cocoanut. He was kept very busy, calling out his call, picking up the balls; and the heap of pennies and sixpences in the lolly drawer grew bigger.

went the music box; Cocoa begged, Nuts frisked, and Candy Floss turned round and round.

When the cocoanuts were all gone Jack would empty the lolly drawer, put out the lights, and close the shy. He shut off the music box and let Cocoa get down. Nuts was covered over with an old red cloth so that he could sleep; Jack put Candy Floss into his pocket (there was a hole handy so that she could see out) and, with Cocoa at his heels, went round the fair.

They went on the big merry-go-rounds where the big steam organs played "Yankee Doodle" and "Colonel Bogey" and other tunes. Jack sat on a horse or a wooden swan, a camel or an elephant, with Cocoa on the saddle in front of him and Candy Floss safe in his pocket; round they went, helter-skelter, until Candy Floss was dizzy. The little merry-go-rounds had buses, engines, and motorcars that were too small for Jack, but sometimes Candy Floss and Cocoa sat in a car by themselves. Here the music was nursery rhymes, and the children tooted the horns. Toot. Toot-toot-toot. Candy Floss wished she could toot a horn.

Sometimes they went to the Bingo booths and tried to win prizes. Once Jack had won a silk handkerchief, bright purple printed with shamrocks in emerald-green. Cocoa and Candy Floss thought it a most beautiful prize and Jack always wore it round his neck.

Sometimes they went on the bumper cars. When the cars bumped into one another the girls shut their eyes and squealed; Candy Floss's eyes would not shut, but she would have liked to squeal.

Best of all they went on the big wheel, with its seats that went up and up in the air high over the fair and the lights, so high that Candy Floss trembled, even though she was in Jack's pocket.

When they were hungry they would eat fair food. Sometimes they ate hot dogs from the hot-dog stall; Cocoa had one to himself but Candy Floss had the tip end of Jack's. Sometimes they had fish and chips at the fried-fish bar; Cocoa had whole fish and Candy Floss had a chip. Often they had toffee apples; Cocoa used to get his stuck on his jaw and had to stand on his head to get it off. Sometimes they had ice cream and Jack made a tiny cone out of a cigarette paper for Candy Floss.

When they were tired they came back to an old van that Jack had bought dirt cheap (which was what he called buying for very little money). He had mended it and now it would go anywhere. Jack put the music box and Nuts in the van too, so that they would all be together. Then he closed the doors and they all lay down to sleep.

Jack slept on the floor of the van on some sacks and an old sleeping bag. Cocoa slept at Jack's feet. Candy Floss slept in the empty lolly drawer which Jack put beside his pillow; the sixpences and pennies had been put in a stocking that Jack kept in a secret place. He folded up the shamrock handkerchief to make the drawer soft for Candy Floss and tucked one end round her for a blanket.

As she lay in the drawer Candy Floss could feel Jack big and warm beside her; she could hear Cocoa breathing, and knew Nuts was under the cloth. Outside, the music of the fair went on; through the van window the stars looked like sixpences. Soon Candy Floss was fast asleep.

Fairs do not stay in one place very long, only a day, two days, perhaps a week. Then Jack would pack up the cocoanut shy, the lights and the flags, the posts, the nuts, the stands, and the wooden balls. He would take down the three-sided tent, put everything on the van, start it up, and drive away. The music box with Nuts traveled on the floor in front, Cocoa sat on the seat, but Candy Floss had the best place of all: Jack made the shamrock handkerchief into a sling for her and hung it on the driving mirror. Candy Floss could watch the road and see everywhere they went.

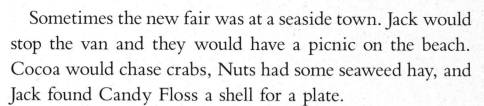

Sometimes the new fair was at a seaside town. Jack would stop the van and they would have a picnic on the beach. Cocoa would chase crabs, Nuts had some seaweed hay, and Jack found Candy Floss a shell for a plate.

Sometimes the fair was in the country and they picnicked in a wood. Cocoa chased rabbits, not crabs, Nuts had moss for straw, and Jack found Candy Floss an acorn cup for a drinking bowl.

Sometimes they stopped in a field. Cocoa would have liked to chase sheep but he did not dare. Jack made daisy-chain reins for Nuts, Candy Floss had a wild rose for a hat; but no matter where they stopped to picnic, sooner or later the van would drive on to another fairground and Jack would put up the shy.

Cocoa would be brushed and his bow put on, and he would get up on his stool while Jack filled the bowl marked "Dog." The cloth came off the music box and Nuts would be polished with a rag until he shone. Then Jack would fluff up Candy Floss's dress and with his own comb spread out her hair. He washed her face (sometimes, I am sorry to say, with spit) and sat her carefully on the saddle and switched on the music and lights. "Three f'r threepence! Seven f'r a tanner!" Jack would cry.

went the music box; Cocoa begged, Nuts frisked, and Candy Floss turned round and round.

Sometimes the other fair people laughed at Jack about what they called his toys; but, "Shut up out of that," he would say. "Toys? They're partners." (Only he said "pardners.")

"A doll for a partner? Garn!" they would jeer.

"Doll! She's my luck," said Jack.

That was true. Jack's shy had more people and took in more pennies and sixpences than any other shy.

Cocoa, Nuts, and Candy Floss were proud to be Jack's partners; Candy Floss was very proud to be his luck.

Then one Easter they came to the heath high up above London which was the biggest fair of all (a heath is a big open space, covered with grass). Only the very best shies and merry-go-rounds, the biggest wheels were there. The Bingos had expensive prizes, there were three rifle ranges, a mouse circus, and stalls where you could smash china. There were toy-sellers and balloon-sellers, paper flowers and paper umbrellas. There were rows and rows of hot-dog stalls, fish bars, and toffee-apple shops.

Cocoa had a new bow. Nuts had new silver bells. Candy Floss had a new pink dress like a cloud. Jack painted the posts and bought a pile of new cocoanuts.

"Goin' to make more lolly'n ever we done," said Jack. "More sixpences 'n stars in the sky."

went the music box; and how well Cocoa begged, how gaily Nuts frisked, and Candy Floss turned round and round as gracefully as a dancer. More and more people began to come—Hundreds of people, thought Candy Floss. The wooden balls flew; pennies and sixpences poured into the lolly drawer.

"That's my luck!" cried Jack, and Candy Floss felt very proud.

25

Now not far from the heath, in a big house on the hill leading down from the heath to the town, there lived a girl called Clementina Davenport.

She was seven years old, with brown hair cut in a fringe, brown eyes, a small straight nose, and a small red mouth. She would have been pretty if she had not looked so cross. She looked cross because she *was* cross. She said she had nothing to do.

"I don't know *what* to do with Clementina," said her mother. "What can I give her to make her happy?"

Clementina had a day nursery and a night nursery all to herself, and a garden to play in. She had a nurse who was not allowed to tell her to sit up or pay attention or eat her pudding or any of the other things you and I are told.

She had a dolls' house, a white piano, cupboards full of toys, and two bookcases filled with books. She had a toy kitten in a basket, a toy poodle in another, and a real kitten and a real poodle as well. She had a cage of budgerigars and a pony to ride. Last Christmas her father gave her a pale blue bicycle, and her mother a watch, a painting box, and a painting book. Still Clementina had nothing to do.

"What *am* I to do with Clementina?" asked her mother, and she gave her a new television set and a pair of roller skates.

You might think Clementina had everything she wanted, but no, she was still quite good at wants and, on Easter Monday afternoon when the garden was full of daffodils and blossom, the sound of the fair came from the heath, over the wall, into the garden; and, "I want to go to the fair," said Clementina.

Another way in which Clementina was not like you or me was that for her "I want" was the same as "I shall."

"*Not* a nasty common fair!" said her mother.

"I *want* to go," said Clementina and stamped her foot, and so her father put on his hat, fetched his walking stick, and took her to the fair.

Of course she went on every-thing: on the little merry-go-rounds where she rode on a bus and wanted to change to an en-gine, then changed to a car and back to the bus; on the big merry-go-rounds where she rode on a swan and changed to a camel and changed to a horse.

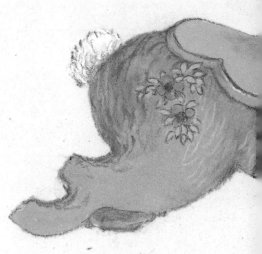

She went on the bumper cars where she did not squeal but was angry when her car was hit; on the swing boats where she did not want to stop; and on the big wheel where she wanted to stop at once and shrieked so that they had to slow it and take her down. She cried at Bingo when she did not win a prize and screamed when the mice ran into the ring in the mouse circus. Her father bought her a toffee apple which she licked once and threw away, a balloon which she burst, and a paper umbrella with which she hit at people's legs.

Having everything you want can make you very tired. When Clementina was tired she whined. "I don't like fairs," whined Clementina, "I want to go home." (Only she said, "I wa-ant to go ho-o-o-ome.")

"Come along then," said her father.

"Fetch the car," said Clementina, but motorcars cannot go into fairs; and, "I'm afraid you will have to walk," said her father.

Clementina was getting ready to cry when she heard a gay loud sound:

and a call, "Three f'r threepence! Seven f'r a tanner!" and she turned round and saw Candy Floss.

She saw Candy Floss sitting on Nuts, turning round and round as Nuts frisked up and down. Clementina saw the red shoes, the pink gauze, the way the blue eyes shone, the gold-spun hair, and, "I want that doll," said Clementina.

People often asked to buy Candy Floss, or Cocoa or Nuts; then Jack would laugh and say, "You'll have to buy me as well. We're pardners," and the people would laugh too, for they knew they could not buy Jack. "Candy Floss? Why, she's my luck, couldn't sell that," Jack would say. "Pretty as a pi'ture, ain't she?" said Jack.

Now Clementina's father came to Jack. "My little girl would like to buy your doll."

"Sorry, sir," said Jack. "Not f'r sale."

"I want her," said Clementina.

"I will give you a pound," said Clementina's father to Jack.

A pound is forty silver sixpences; but, "Not f'r five hundred pounds," said Jack.

"You see, Clementina," said her father.

"Give him five hundred pounds," said Clementina.

Her father walked away and Jack smiled at Clementina. "I said *not* f'r five hundred pounds, little missy."

I cannot tell you how furious was Clementina. She scowled at Jack (scowl means to make an ugly face). Jack stepped closer to Candy Floss and Cocoa growled; and, "You cut along to yer pa," said Jack to Clementina. Jack, of course, treated her as if she were any little girl, and she did not like that.

She made herself as tall as she could and said, "Do you know who I am? I am Clementina Davenport."

"And I'm Jack and these are Cocoa, Nuts, and Candy Floss," said Jack.

"I am Clementina Davenport," said Clementina scornfully. "I live in a big house. I have a room full of toys and a pony. I have a bicycle and twenty pairs of shoes."

"That's nice f'r you," said Jack, "but you can't have Candy Floss."

I believe that was the first time anyone had ever said "can't" to Clementina.

Jack thought he had settled it. In any case he was too busy picking up balls, taking in pennies and sixpences, handing out cocoanuts, and calling his call to pay much attention to Clementina. "Cut off," he told her, but Clementina did not cut off. She came nearer.

Cocoa, Nuts, and Candy Floss watched her out of the corners of their eyes.

Clementina was pretending not to be interested, but she came nearer still. If Candy Floss and Nuts had been breathing they would have held their breath.

Clementina came close and at that moment Cocoa got down to take a lap of water from his bowl. (It was not Cocoa's fault; he had never known a girl like Clementina.)

Nuts tried to turn faster, but he could only turn as fast as the music went. He wanted to kick, but he had to hold his forelegs up; he tried to shake his silver bells, but they did not make enough noise.

As Clementina's hand came out Candy Floss shrieked, "Help! Help!" but a doll's shriek has no sound. She tried to cling like a burr to the saddle, but she was too small.

When Jack turned round Candy Floss had gone. There was no sign of Clementina.

When Clementina snatched Candy Floss, quick-as-a-cat-can-wink-its-eye she hid her in the paper umbrella and ran after her father.

Candy Floss was head-downward, which made her dizzy. The umbrella banged against Clementina's legs as she ran and that gave Candy Floss great bumps. She trembled with terror as she felt herself being carried far away; but she had not been brought up in a fair for nothing. She was used to being dizzy (on the merry-go-rounds), used to being bumped (on the bumper cars), used to trembling (on the big wheel), and when, in the big house on the hill, Clementina took her out of the umbrella Candy Floss looked almost as pretty and calm as she had on Nuts's saddle; but china can be cold and hard; she made herself cold and hard in Clementina's hand and her eyes looked as if they were the brightest, clearest glass.

Dolls cannot talk aloud; they talk in wishes. You and I have often felt them wish and we know how clear that can be, but Clementina had never played long enough with any of her dolls to feel a wish. She had never felt anything at all.

"But you will," said Candy Floss, "you will."

Clementina turned all her dolls'-house dolls out of the dolls' house, higgledy-piggledy onto the floor. "You will live in the dolls' house," she told Candy Floss.

"I live in a cocoanut shy," said Candy Floss and her dress caught on the prim little chairs and tables and her hair caught on the shells that edged the scrap-pictures. Every time Clementina moved her she upset something. When she had knocked down a lamp, spilled a vase of flowers, and pulled the cloth off a table, Clementina took her out.

"Don't live in the dolls' house then," said Clementina.

"You must wear another dress," said Clementina and tried to take the pink one off, but she did not know, as Jack knew, how to soften the glue. All she did was to tear the gauze. Then she tried to put another dress over the top of the gauze skirt, but it stuck out and Candy Floss made her arms so stiff they would not go in the sleeves. Clementina lost patience and threw the dress on the floor.

She made a charming supper for Candy Floss: a daisy poached egg, some green grass spinach, and a blossom fruit salad with paint sauce. She had never taken such trouble over a supper before, but Candy Floss would not touch it.

"I eat hot dogs," said Candy Floss, "a chip, or a toffee apple." Nor would she take any notice of the dolls' house's best blue and white china. "I eat off a shell," said Candy Floss. "I drink from an acorn bowl."

"Eat it up," said Clementina, but Candy Floss tumbled slowly forward onto the supper and lay with her face in the blossom fruit salad.

"I shall put you to bed," scolded Clementina and she got out the dolls'-house bed.

"I don't sleep in a bed," said Candy Floss, "I sleep in a lolly drawer," and she made herself stiff so that her feet stuck out. When Clementina tucked them in, Candy Floss's head stuck out. Clementina put the bedclothes round her but they sprang up again at once. "Are you trying to fight me?" asked Clementina.

Candy Floss did not answer, but the bedclothes sprang up again.

"Well, you can sit on a chair all night," said Clementina and she took out a dolls'-house chair.

"I don't sit on a chair," said Candy Floss, "I sit on Nuts," and as soon as Clementina put her on the chair she fell off.

"*Sit!*" said Clementina in a terrible voice, but a doll

brought up in the noise and shouts of a fair is not to be frightened by a little girl's voice and Candy Floss did not blink an eye. "Sit!" said Clementina and she sat Candy Floss hard on the chair. *Snap,* the chair legs broke.

Clementina stood looking at the pieces in her hand; she looked as if she were thinking. And if Candy Floss's little china mouth had not been smiling already, I should have said she smiled.

But she did not smile in the night. Clementina left her on the table when she went to bed and all night long Candy Floss lay on the cold table in that strange room.

There was no van; no music box with Nuts asleep under the old red cloth; no sound of Cocoa breathing; no Jack to feel big and warm; no lolly drawer to make a bed; no shamrock handkerchief. There was no music from the fair, no sixpence stars.

"And how can I get back?" asked Candy Floss. "I *can't* get back. Oh, how will the shy go on? What will Jack do without his luck?" And all night the frightening words beat in her head: "No luck. No luck. No Jack. No luck. No Nuts or Cocoa. No sixpences. No luck! No luck! No luck!"

Dolls cannot cry but they can feel. In the night Candy Floss felt so much she thought that she must crack.

39

Next morning it began again. Clementina took Candy Floss into the garden. "You must go in my dolls'-house perambulator," said Clementina.

"I go in a pocket," said Candy Floss, and she would not fit in the perambulator. She held her head up so that it would not go under the hood and made her legs stiff so that they would not go in either. Clementina shook her until her eyes came loose in her head.

"You belong to me now," said Clementina.

"I belong to Jack."

Candy Floss, as we know, could not say these things aloud, but now Clementina was beginning to feel them. Clementina was not used to feeling; the more she felt, the angrier she grew, and she thought of something dreadful to say to Candy Floss. "Pooh!" said Clementina. "You're only a doll. The shops are full of dolls. Jack will have another doll by now. Do you think he wouldn't have bought another doll to take your place?"

Candy Floss seemed to sway in Clementina's hand. Another doll in her place! In all her places! On Nuts's back; in Jack's pocket; in the lolly drawer; in the shamrock handkerchief. Another doll to be Jack's luck! What shall I do? thought Candy Floss. What can I do? And she cried out with such a big wish that she fell out of Clementina's hand onto the path and a crack ran down her back. "Jack! Jack! Cocoa! Nuts! Help! Help! Help!" cried Candy Floss.

At that moment, in the fair, the merry-go-rounds started up.

All the merry-go-rounds up and down the heath began to play. The big wheel started and the rifles cracked in the rifle ranges. People began to cry "Bingo!" and the toy-sellers and balloon-sellers started to shout. All the music in the fair began to play, louder and louder, until it sounded as if the whole fair were in the garden.

Clementina picked Candy Floss up off the path, and what had happened? Candy Floss was cracked; her eyes were loose, the shine had gone out of her hair, her face was covered with paint where she had fallen into the salad, and her dress was torn. As for its pink, you know how brown and dull pink spun sugar can go. Candy Floss's dress looked just like that.

"You're horrid," said Clementina and she threw Candy Floss back onto the path.

The merry-go-round and the fair music seemed to say that too, "You're horrid," but they were saying it to Clementina.

"I think I shall go indoors and paint," said Clementina. She went in but the fair music came into the house and now, as Clementina listened, she heard other things as well. "She belongs to Jack." "You're horrid." "Cruel Clementina," said the music.

"I won't sit still. I shall skip," said Clementina, but though she skipped up to a hundred times she could not shut out that music. "She belongs to Jack." "Cruel Clementina." "Poor Candy Floss"; and the big wheel turning — you could see the top of it from the garden — seemed to say, "I can see. I can see everything."

When lunchtime came Clementina did not want any lunch. "Are you ill?" asked the nurse and made Clementina lie down on her bed with a picture book. "You look quite bad," said the nurse.

"I don't!" shouted Clementina and hid under her blanket because that was what she did not want to feel, bad; but the bed and the picture book, even the blanket, could not shut out the fair, and the music never stopped: "Bad Clementina." "Cruel Clementina." "She belongs to Jack." "Poor Candy Floss."

Clementina put her head under the pillow.

Under the pillow she could not hear the music but she heard something else: thumpity-bump; thumpity-bump; it was her own heart beating. Clementina had not known she had a heart before; now it thumped just like the merry-go-round engine, and what was it saying? "Poor Candy Floss. Poor Candy Floss," inside Clementina.

She lay very still. She was listening. Then she began to cry.

By and by Clementina sat up. She got out of bed and put on her shoes; then, just as she was, rumpled and crumpled from lying on the bed and tear-stained from crying, she tiptoed out of the room and went down the stairs into the garden, where she picked up Candy Floss and she tiptoed to the gate.

No one was about. She opened the gate and ran.

She ran up the hill to the heath and into the fair, past the balloon-man and the toy-sellers, the fish-and-chips bar, the hot-dog stands and the toffee-apple stalls. She ran past the little merry-go-rounds with the buses and cars, and the big merry-go-rounds with the horses and swans, past the Bingos, the mouse circus, the rifle ranges, and the big wheel . . . and then she stopped.

The cocoanut shy was closed.

No lights shone; no cocoanuts were set up on the red and white posts. The balls were stacked in their scarlet stands. The music box was covered with the old red cloth. Nuts could not be seen. Cocoa lay on the ground with his head on his paws; now and again he whimpered.

Jack was sitting on a box, hunched and still. When people came to the shy he shook his head. "My luck's gone," he said, and Cocoa put up his nose and howled.

Clementina had meant to put Candy Floss back on Nuts and then run away as fast as she could, but she could not bear it when she saw how miserable she had made them all. She could not bear to see Nuts covered up, Cocoa whimpering, Jack's sad face; and, without thinking or waiting, she cried, "Oh *please,* don't be so sorry! I have brought her back."

Jack stood up. Cocoa stood up. The cloth slithered off the music box and there was Nuts, standing up. "Brought her *back?*" asked Jack, and Clementina forgot all about being Clementina Davenport in the big house on the hill; and, "Yes, I'm Clementina. I took her," she said and burst into tears.

When Jack saw what Clementina had done to Candy Floss he looked very, very grave and Cocoa growled; but Jack was used to mending things and in no time at all he had borrowed some china cement from the china-smashing stall and filled in the crack. He would not let Clementina hold Candy Floss but he let her watch, though Cocoa still growled softly under his breath. Very gently he touched the loosened eyes with glue and made them firm again. He washed the torn skirt off and glued a fresh one on and cleaned the paint off Candy Floss's face; then he spun out her hair again and she looked as good as new. Cocoa stopped growling and Clementina actually smiled.

Then in a jiffy (which was what Jack called a moment) he put fresh cocoanuts on the posts and opened the ball stands. He put Cocoa's bow on and told him to jump up on the stool; he ran over Nuts's paint with a rag so that it shone; then he put Candy Floss in the saddle and switched on the music box.

went the music box.

"Three balls f'r threepence! Seven f'r a tanner!" called Jack. His shout sounded so joyful, Cocoa begged so cleverly, Nuts frisked so happily, and Candy Floss turned so gaily that the crowds flocked to the shy. "Come 'n help!" called Jack to Clementina and Clementina began to pick up the balls.

But who was this coming? It was Clementina's father and mother and with them the nurse and all the maids and a policeman, because there had been *such* a fuss when they had missed Clementina. They had searched all through the fair. Now they stopped at the cocoanut shy.

"Is *that* Clementina?" asked her father and mother, the nurse and the maids.

The cross look had gone from Clementina's face; she was

too busy to be cross. Her cheeks were as pink as Candy Floss's dress; her eyes were shining as if they were made of glass; her hair looked almost gold.

"*Can* it be Clementina?" asked her father and mother, the nurse and the maids.

"Clementina, Clementina!" they called, amazed.

"Three f'r threepence! Seven f'r a tanner!" yelled Clementina.

"What *am* I to do with her?" cried her mother.

It was the policeman who answered, the policeman who had been called out to look for Clementina. "If I was you, mum," said the policeman, "I should leave her alone."

Clementina was allowed to stay all afternoon at the shy. Her father and mother thought it was they who allowed her; Jack thought it was Jack. She worked so hard picking up balls that he gave her two sixpences for herself, and Clementina was prouder of those sixpences than of all the pound notes in her money box (she calls it a lolly box now). "I *earned* them," said Clementina.

When her nurse came to take her home she had to say good-by to Jack, Cocoa, Nuts, and Candy Floss; but, "Not good-by; so long," said Jack.

"So long?" asked Clementina.

"So long as there's fairs we'll be back," said Jack. "Come 'n look f'r us."

When Clementina was in bed and happily asleep the fair went on.

went the music box.

"Three f'r threepence! Seven f'r a tanner!" called Jack. Cocoa begged, Nuts frisked, and Candy Floss went round and round.